NORTHERN
AGGRESSION

Northern Aggression

ISBN-13: 978-1944540159
ISBN-10: 1944540156

For information about production rights, visit:
www.jzettelmaier.com

Published by Sordelet Ink
Cover by David Blixt

Northern Aggression

Originally Titled
And The Creek Don't Rise

A Play By
Joseph Zettelmaier

Published by
*S*ordelet Ink

NORTHERN AGGRESSION (originally entitled AND THE CREEK DON'T RISE) received its world premiere on July 7, 2011 at Williamston Theatre. It was directed by Joseph Albright. Set Design by Daniel C. Walker, Lighting Design by Reid G. Johnson, Costume Design by Holly Iler, Sound Design by Will Myers. The production was stage managed by Nan Luchini.

The cast was as follows:

ROB GRAFF: John Lepard
MADDIE GRAFF: Kate Peckham
DOC BOGGS: Thomas D. Mahard

Cast of Characters

ROB GRAFF - an unemployed automotive engineer, 45
MADDIE GRAFF - his wife, a veterinarian, 30
DR. BENJAMIN "DOC" BOGGS - a retired physician, 70s

Time
The Present

Place
Various locations in Carson, Georgia

ACT I

SCENE 1

(The kitchen of ROB & MADDIE's new house. It is set up-tables, chairs, etc. MADDIE is checking everything out. ROB can be heard offstage shouting)

MADDIE
Honey?! What is...

(ROB rushes onstage, holding a large suitcase)

ROB
Oh my god. I just...oh god...it was...

MADDIE
What was it?

ROB
Like a rat...except huge...possibly prehistoric...

MADDIE
Just slow down.

ROB
You should've seen this thing! It was...like...

(He spreads out his hands, showing her how large the animal was) And it hissed!

MADDIE
Hissed? Like a snake?

ROB
No! Like some sort of demon-rat! Get me a gun and a bible.

MADDIE
Rob. Rob.

ROB
Yeah?

MADDIE
Was it a possum?

ROB
No! It was...I don't know.

MADDIE
Grey. Hairless tail. Close-together eyes?

ROB
Yes! Prehistoric demon rat!

MADDIE
Honey, that was a possum.

ROB
That's a possum?

MADDIE
Don't worry. They're harmless. It just hissed because you scared it.

ROB
No, no, no. It hissed to scare me. I'm very confident about that.

MADDIE
Stay here. I'll take care of it. *(She heads off)*

ROB
No! Trust me! That thing is looking for a fight!

MADDIE
I've got this. *(She can be heard offstage)*Go on! Go! Get out of here! *(After a moment, she returns)* The possum says you scream like a girl.

(He laughs)

ROB
Please just tell me it's not living here.

MADDIE
It ran into a burrow across the street. I think it was just investigating. You've really never seen one before?

ROB
Yeah. On the Discovery Channel, I think. *(Beat)* So let's just load everything back into the car and get out of here.

MADDIE
Rob...

ROB
No, no. The possum has clearly marked his territory. I say we just give him the house and cut our losses.

MADDIE
You're hilarious. *(She goes to him, hugs him)*

ROB
New rule - you have to deal with the wildlife.

MADDIE
That's fair.

ROB
I'll handle the home-repair, you handle the giant rodents.

MADDIE
It's a marsupial, actually.

ROB
Show off. *(Beat. ROB looks around the room)* Wait. This place looks different.

MADDIE
Is it because we've got everything moved in?

(He stares at her, shocked & thrilled)

ROB
We're moved in?

MADDIE
We're moved in.

(She runs at him, jumping up. He catches her)

ROB
Careful. I stink.

MADDIE
I don't care. I do not care. We're unpacked.

ROB
Yes we are. *(He kisses her, then sets her down)*

MADDIE
How's your back, old man?

ROB
It's fine. *(He sits down tenderly in a chair. She stares at him)* It's fine.

MADDIE
Uh-huh.

ROB
This is not my back. This is an old baseball injury.

MADDIE
Located in your back.

ROB
It's an amazing coincidence.

MADDIE
Pansy. *(She rubs his shoulders. He winces in pain)* Too hard?

ROB
Yeah.

MADDIE
Want some ice?

ROB
No, just... *(He rises, then lies down on the table)* Oh yeah. There we go.

MADDIE
I threw your back out.

ROB
No, no, no. No. It's from moving.

MADDIE
Am I getting heavy?

ROB
Oh dear lord...

MADDIE
'Cause you can tell me if I am.

(Beat)

ROB
You're getting heavy.

(She hits him. He laughs)

ROB
See?! You told me I could tell you, but you lied.

MADDIE
It's the damn food here! You don't know! I was here for a month before you got here. You don't know what it was like. Set up the office, go to the Chic-Fillet. Meet with the staff, go to Krystals. It's all fat, Rob. It looks like meat, like vegetables, but it's all fat. And the next thing I know, I...

ROB
(taking her hand) Honey, I was joking. You're like 110 pounds. No one anywhere, ever, would call that heavy.

MADDIE
Oh! New rule-If you make fun of my weight, I can make fun of your age.

ROB
Sure. Why not? *(He rises and heads offstage)*

MADDIE
Where are you going?

ROB
Tylenol.

(They continue talking, though he remains offstage)

MADDIE
Know what you need?

ROB
Tylenol?

MADDIE
You need to get out. Check out the town.

ROB
This isn't a town. It's where culture goes to die.

MADDIE
Come on.

ROB
…churches and antique stores as far as the eye can see…

MADDIE
Could you try, for like a second, to pretend you're happy here?

ROB
(Returning, waving his arms and using a silly voice)
Woooo! Look at me! I'm Happy Rob, the world's greatest house husband!

MADDIE
Stop it.

ROB
I hope the girls at the book club like my new sundress!

MADDIE
Rob. Stop.

(Beat)

ROB
(Hurt) You used to like it when I did my stupid voice.

MADDIE
This isn't a joke.

ROB
OK. Sorry.

MADDIE
I just...aren't you at all excited about this? We
have a house. We have a new life.

ROB
See, that's the...you say that like there was something wrong with our old life.

MADDIE
You want me to make a list?

ROB
Ah, Jesus....

MADDIE
One...

ROB
Maddie, don't...

MADDIE
One - we were living in a condo half this size for
twice as much.

ROB
I know. I....

MADDIE
Two - Said condo got broken into twice TWICE
last year alone.

ROB
That could happen anywhere!

MADDIE
Three - You were unemployed, and I...

ROB
OK! I'm still unemployed!

MADDIE
But I'm not! No one in Michigan was making me the kind of offer I have now.

ROB
I know.

MADDIE
We made a sacrifice. I get that. But...God, isn't it worth it?

ROB
I don't know.

(Beat)

MADDIE
What exactly does that mean?

ROB
It means I've been here for a day. You've been here for a month. You can't expect me to be completely adjusted.

MADDIE
Ok. That's fair.

ROB
Ok.

MADDIE
Ok.

(ROB sits down. She joins him, laying her head on his shoulder)

MADDIE
Think of this like a vacation. Relax. Have some fun.

ROB
(Kisses her) I'm gonna be OK. Really. I'm just a little disconnected.

MADDIE
You need friends.

ROB
I have you.

MADDIE
You need guy friends.

ROB
You could wear a moustache and pretend to be a guy friend.

(She just stares at him)

ROB
Nope. Bad idea.

MADDIE
There's a social this weekend. We should go.

ROB
A social?

MADDIE
You know. Like a…a social.

ROB
You have no idea what that is.

MADDIE
I know that there will be people there. People from town. They'll want to meet us.

ROB
I'm sure.

MADDIE
Really. The last month...I've been stopped like three times at the supermarket. Total strangers coming up, asking me if I'm the veterinarian.

ROB
How did they know that?

MADDIE
Small towns. People talk.

ROB
Wonderful.

MADDIE
This is our home now. It's time to make friends.

ROB
I get the distinct impression these people do not want to be our friends.

MADDIE
Not true.

ROB
What about that good ol' boy at the gas station? He just kept staring at our license plate, then at his gun rack.

MADDIE
He did not.

ROB
I swear to God! There was this moment where I was like "Do these people think the Civil War's still going on?"

MADDIE
You're reading too much into it.

(The doorbell rings. MADDIE goes to get it. DOC is standing there in full Southern General uniform. He has a small box in his hand)

DOC
I hope I'm not interrupting anything.

(They just stare at him)

MADDIE
I'm sorry. Are you lost?

DOC
Oh, not at all. I'm y'all's neighbor.

MADDIE
We have neighbors?

DOC
Ha! Isn't that something. Yes, I just live right 'round that bend.

ROB
I didn't see any houses out there for like a mile.

DOC
1.8 miles. That would be me. Benjamin Wilford Boggs. Most folks 'round here call me Doc.

ROB
You're a doctor?

DOC
No, I'm a place you tie your boat. Ha! 'Course I am, son. 'Course I am.

ROB
Well, I'm...

DOC
Retired 4 years now. Had my own private practice for 30 before that. Lord, I do miss it sometimes but...*(Pause. He offers ROB his hand)* Well, listen to me go on. Doc Boggs. Who might you be?

ROB
Rob Graff. This is my wife, Maddie.

MADDIE
Pleased to meet you.

(They shake hands. DOC smiles, taking in their accents)

DOC
Where y'all from, exactly?

MADDIE
Detroit.

DOC
(Laughing loudly) Bless my soul, I've got me some genuine Yankees for neighbors. Isn't that something. Wilson's gonna love this.

ROB
Wilson?

DOC
Hasn't he showed up yet? Well, give him a day or two. He's got the rheumatism, you know? Up in his joints. Not so fast as he used to be. Why, I remember back in...oh, it would have to be '68...Wilson used to be the fastest runner old Carson High'd ever seen. Man could jump anything...and I do mean anything. Hurtles, fences...one time, I saw him jump clear over a 1960 Rambler Rebel. Damndest thing. Oh,

back then, we weren't driving around SUVs or whathaveyou. I suppose jumpin' over one of those monsters would really be something to see.

MADDIE
Excuse me. I'm really sorry. Who's Wilson?

DOC
Lord, where's my head today? Wilson Hadley. President of the Carson Welcoming Committee.

ROB
There's a Welcoming Committee?

DOC
Oh, yes, yes. He's probably just a little behind today, trying to get everything set for the battle.

(Beat)

ROB
There's a battle?

(DOC just stares at him, uncertain what he means. Then he suddenly laughs loudly)

DOC
For the Recreationists! The Civil War Recreationists!

MADDIE
Of course.

DOC
Oh lord, I don't want to even guess what you were thinking.

ROB
No, you probably don't.

DOC
Probably thought Old Doc Boggs had plum fallen off his rocker.

ROB
And there it is.

DOC
Lemme guess, lemme guess. You think I got the entire Light Infantry camped out in your back yard.

ROB
Not the entire Light Infantry, no.

DOC
Ha! Boy, you're a funny one, and don't let anybody tell you otherwise. *(He hands them the package)*

MADDIE
Oh. Thank you! What's this?

DOC
Just a little somethin' to say "Welcome to Carson, Georgia-Prettiest little town you're ever likely to meet."

(She opens it. It's full of jarred preserves)

ROB
What's in there, hon?

DOC
That'd be Doc Boggs's famous Peach Preserves. What you want to do is toast up an English muffin, then spread 'em on top. You'll think you died and gone to heaven.

MADDIE
That is so sweet!

DOC
I'd hope so. They're made with my own peaches.

MADDIE
No, I meant...

DOC
I know what you meant, darlin'. I was just funnin'
with you.

*(There is a beat, as no one is entirely certain how to
keep the conversation moving)*

MADDIE
Your costume is amazing.

DOC
Thank you, Madeline. That's right kind. But it's
not a costume. It's a uniform.

MADDIE
Oh. I'm sorry.

DOC
Not at all.

*(They notice he's been pulling on a tear in his coat
jacket)*

ROB
Hey, not sure if you know it, but you've got a tear
there.

DOC
Beg pardon?

ROB
On your...costu...um...grey jacket.

DOC
Oh yes, of course. Wouldn't you know it. I was

trying it on for tomorrow, and damn if I didn't catch my arm on a loose nail. *(Holds up his coat. The arm is torn on the seam)* Actually, I must confess to a bit of duplicity on my part. My visit wasn't entirely motivated by neighborly kindness.

ROB
OK

DOC
Miss Madeline, might you know your way around a thread and needle?

MADDIE
Oh.

DOC
If it's not an inconvenience. After all, General Braxton Bragg shouldn't show up to the battle threadbare.

MADDIE
Oh. Of course. Right. It's just...I don't really sew.

DOC
You don't?

MADDIE
I don't.

DOC
Not even a little?

MADDIE
Not really. I mean, sutures. But that's about it.

DOC
Well I'll be.

ROB
Weird, right? A woman who can't sew. And still I

married her.

MADDIE
Rob can sew.

DOC
What?

ROB
Hold on.

MADDIE
He can! He even taught a Home Economics class through the Rec & Ed.

(ROB stares at her. Clearly he doesn't feel this should be public knowledge)

ROB
I...I have three sisters.

DOC
Oh. I see. *(Beat)* Well, I don't...that is...would you perhaps...

ROB
Lemme take a look at it.

(DOC hands him the coat. ROB examines it)

ROB
Oh, this is nothing.

DOC
Then it's repairable?

ROB
Yeah. Gimme a few minutes.

DOC
Sir, you are a gentleman and a seamstr...oh. I'm...not entirely certain what one calls a male

seamstress.

ROB
A tailor.

DOC
Oh. Yes, of course. That certainly...yes.

(ROB heads off)

MADDIE
Would you like something to drink?

DOC
Well now, I'll tell you, I'd be very grateful for a glass of sweet tea.

MADDIE
Oh. I think all we have is water and Pepsi.

DOC
Water would be lovely.

MADDIE
We're just moving in and... Actually, I've been living here for a month. Rob was in Michigan finishing up the sale. Of our old house.

DOC
Well, you've found yourself a fine new home and that's God's honest truth. The Abeline's...they lived here before y'all, you know...they took real good care of this house. I helped them move in. Did you know that?

MADDIE
No.

DOC
Oh yes, this would've been...let me see...oh, 1970 or thereabouts. Mr. Abeline, he came up from

Savannah to be the new superintendant. Filmore,
that was his name. Filmore Abeline. Don't that
beat all?

(MADDIE laughs)

DOC
Well, he and his wife Katy lived here 'til 2005,
I believe it was. She passed away, you see. Bad
ticker. He moved back to Savannah after that. Not
really certain what he's up to there. Filmore and
I weren't overly close, you see.

MADDIE
Really?

DOC
Oh, I'm afraid so. We had something of a
disagreement as to where his property line
ended and mine began. But I can already tell
I'm gonna get along with you Michiganders
just fine. Yes, sir. And let me just say, I apolo-
gize for not visiting sooner. I kept meaning
to stop by, but the days just slipped away from
me, I reckon.

MADDIE
My mom calls it Southern Time.

DOC
How's that?

MADDIE
She's from Virginia. She says "however long you
think something should take, double it. That's
how Southern Time works."

DOC
Southern time! I like that, Madeline! I surely do!
She's from Virginia, you say?

MADDIE
Yeah. Danville.

DOC
Why, that must be why I took such a shine to you.
You've got rebel blood in your veins.

MADDIE
I guess so.

DOC
Wonderful history up in Virginia. I myself am
partial to the First Battle of Bull Run.

*(She doesn't respond, as she isn't overly familiar with
the topic)*

DOC
I suppose y'all might call it The Battle of Manassas.
(DOC reads her expression and smiles) There I go
again. I beg your pardon, Madeline. The War of
Northern Aggression is a passion of mine. Just ask
Barksdale.

MADDIE
Who's Barksdale?

DOC
He is the last in a line of proud, purebred British
Bulldogs that have been in my family since the
60s. He's 13 years old now, but a better friend
I couldn't ask for. And named after the famous
Confederate General William Barksdale.

MADDIE
Oh! I love bulldogs!

DOC
Do you now?

MADDIE
I'm a veterinarian, actually.

DOC
You're the one who replaced old George Hathaway,
am I correct?

MADDIE
You are correct.

DOC
Well, if you don't mind my saying, you're a far
sight prettier than George.

MADDIE
I don't mind at all.

(Beat)

DOC
Now where was I again?

MADDIE
Bulldogs? Or the Re-enactments?

DOC
Oh! Yes! The Re-enactments, they're very popular 'round these parts. We Georgians take that sort
of thing very seriously. It's half historical recre-
ation, half social club. Y'all should come to one
of our battles.

MADDIE
I didn't realize people could just...go to those.

DOC
Oh yes, it's quite the to-do. What you want to do
is pack yourself a nice picnic lunch and drag your
husband to the battlefield. After the smoke clears,
I'll introduce y'all around.

MADDIE
Oh my god. You would do that?

DOC
It would be my pleasure.

MADDIE
It's just...we don't know anyone here, really. Rob's having a hard time adjusting. He's been trying to find a job and...

DOC
He's unemployed, you say?

MADDIE
Yeah. He's getting discouraged, I think. Don't tell him I said that, but...

DOC
Your secret is safe with me, darlin'.

MADDIE
We need to spend more time in town, you know? It'll help us...

DOC
Don't you say another word. Old Doc Boggs is working out a plan as we speak.

(ROB returns with the jacket)

ROB
Here you go.

DOC
(Inspecting it) Well, bless my soul! Would you look at that! My mother couldn't have done a better job herself. Robert, you have my thanks.

ROB
No problem. And you can call me...

DOC
Robert, I am having a thought.

ROB
Oh. Um…good?

DOC
My thought is this. Have you ever handled a rifle before?

(Beat)

ROB
I was an engineer.

DOC
Is that a no?

ROB
I mean, my dad took me hunting a couple of…

DOC
Wonderful! It just so happens that our James Longstreet got himself the gout. His big toe is the size of a bowling ball. How would you like to join the South in glorious battle?

(Beat)

ROB
I mostly watch hockey.

MADDIE
Honey, I think Doc is asking you to join the recreationists.

ROB
Oh. Yeah. It's ok. I mean, thank you, but…

DOC
It just so happens that most of Carson's City

Fathers are re-enactors, just like yours truly. You're just about Carl Rossom's size...Carl was our Longstreet, don't you know. Yes, yes. This is providence at work.

ROB
I've never really done anything like that before.

DOC
Don't you worry about a thing. I'll be there the whole time, walking you 'round the curves.

ROB
It's just that we just moved in and...

MADDIE
He'll do it.

(ROB *stares at her. She stares back*)

ROB
I think I just got drafted.

DOC
Wonderful! I tell you what I'll do. I'll drop by tomorrow and give you Carl's uniform. Then y'all come to Peachtree Park round about noon, and I'll give you the benefit of my knowledge.

MADDIE
Sounds like a plan.

DOC
Trust me, Robert. You will not regret this.

ROB
I'm choosing to believe that.

DOC
Well, I'll leave you to your settlin' in. Until tomorrow, then. Madeline. Robert. (*Turns to go*) Ha!

Those Yankees won't know what hit 'em! *(Exits)*

(ROB just stares at MADDIE)

ROB
What the hell just happened?

(Lights change)

Scene 2

(DOC & ROB, outdoors, are in full Confederate outfits. ROB's doesn't fit as well as it could. DOC is quizzing ROB on his information)

DOC
So you understand?

ROB
I understand.

DOC
This is a key moment in the Battle of Chickamauga. Rosencrans has ordered the general retreat, and we're gonna take the field. The victory is due to the actions of...

ROB
Of the left wing.

DOC
Exactly. Denied reinforcements from the failed right wing, we will lead the left wing to Snodgrass Hill and...

ROB
I know!

DOC
I know, SIR.

ROB
What?

DOC
I am your commanding officer. You shall address me as "sir."

(Beat. ROB mumbles something under his breath)

DOC
I'm gonna assume there was a "sir" in there.

ROB
That's a fantastic assumption.

DOC
Something got you riled, boy?

ROB
Sorry, I'm surrounded by men with guns. It makes me edgy.

DOC
I told you. They're firing blanks. They're harmless.

ROB
Yes, sir.

DOC
Unless you get shot in the face. Or at very close range.

(ROB stares at him)

DOC
Don't worry. I'm a doctor. You won't die under my command.

ROB
I'm going home.

DOC
And let those damned Yankees take Snodgrass Hill! Never!

ROB
I'm a damn...!

(ROB realizes others are looking at him. He speaks quietly to DOC)

ROB
I'm a damn Yankee.

DOC
Not today, you're not. Today you are...

ROB
General James Longstreet, commander of the Left Wing.

DOC
Lieutenant General James Longstreet.

ROB
Right.

DOC
Son, if you want to make inroads with the city fathers, trust me. This is the side you want to be on.

ROB
I feel like these guys want to slide a bayonet into my spleen.

DOC
Now, to be fair, if you're gonna bayonet someone, you want to hit a lung. It'll drop them
faster.

(ROB stares at DOC)

DOC
I'm sure you'll be fine.

(The sound of a gunshot. ROB jumps)

ROB
What the hell was that?!

DOC
Oh, one of Polk's boys got jumpy. *(Calls off)*
Henry! Keep your pants on or I'll staple them
to your ass! *(To ROB)* That's Henry Buckner. He
runs Buckner Chevrolet. Good man, good man.
He's playing Lt. General Leonidas Polk, who...

ROB
That sounded like a real gun!

DOC
Well, it's supposed to. Why are you getting' so
agitated? You're from Detroit aren't you?

ROB
What the hell is that supposed to mean?

DOC
Now then. We've only got a few minutes before
the battle starts. This is fairly basic re-enacting.
Your men know that you're just a ringer, so they're
gonna go through their maneuvers on their own.
You just stay by me and wave that saber when I
tell you to.

ROB
Fine.

DOC
There's gonna be a lot of gunfire and shouting. And some horseback work. And some simulated cannonfire. Don't let it spook you.

ROB
I don't spook that easy.

DOC
Son, you nearly defecated from the sound of a blank-firing pistol.

ROB
I wasn't ready for it. That's all.

DOC
Then hush up and listen. When I sound the charge, the men are gonna run up there and take on three Yankee regiments. The 21st Ohio, the 89th Ohio, and the 22nd Michigan.

ROB
Wait. We're fighting a Michigan regiment?

DOC
Did I not mention that?

ROB
No, you did not mention that.

DOC
Well, it's not overly important. This is a decisive Confederate victory. Our men are gonna charge the hill, on your order. We'll catch the Union with their pants down and give them the spanking of a lifetime. They're just gonna roll over and take it, like they're supposed to.

(ROB is clearly taking offense to this, and is fighting to keep his mouth shut)

DOC
All you gotta do is wave your sword, give the order, and watch us send those Union bastards straight to black, burning Hell. Got it?

ROB
Oh, I'm getting it.

DOC
Good. *(Sees someone motioning to him in the distance. He nods in response)* All right. It's time. Now - What is Doc Bogg's #1 rule of Re-Enactment?

ROB
Don't get shot in the face?

DOC
There's no time for your addle-pated jibes, boy! WHAT IS THE #1 RULE!?

ROB
Above all else, do not alter the outcome of the battle!

DOC
Yes! Yes! That's the spirit! Now, let's go slaughter those Michiganders!

(The sounds of the troops getting ready, drums & fifes. DOC addresses his troops)

DOC
Proud sons of Georgia, the day is ours! Due to the inept leadership of our opponents, a hole has opened in their ranks; A hole that we shall press through, and deliver final and lasting defeat to the great oppressors!

ROB
(quietly, to himself) Oh come on.

DOC
Remember this day, you brave soldiers all! For on this day, you shall raise your eyes to the Lord Our Creator and say "We are Georgia! We shall stand tall against unjust law and suffer no invader to sully our land!" Let them look into our eyes, and know their own defeat! Let the mighty Chickamauga flow red with the blood of the enemy! And let us praise God who lifted us... TO VICTORY! FOR GEORGIA!

(The troops cheer in response. DOC nudges ROB to sound the attack. ROB half-heartedly swings his saber)

ROB
Go get 'em.

(Trumpets sound. The sound of the Army charging forward, and battle starting. ROB starts getting jumpy)

DOC
Settle down, son. You're more nervous than a long-tailed cat on a porch full of rockin' chairs.

(A cannon goes off)

ROB
Jesus Christ!

DOC
My god, but don't it get your blood flowin'! *(Calls off)* Shore up the line, boys! Here they come!

ROB
Here they...?! They're coming here!?

DOC
This here's what you call a counter-attack.

(More battle sounds as the Union forces press forward. DOC takes out his saber. ROB jumps again)

ROB
What do we do? What do I do?!

DOC
You show some gumption, boy! And leave the orders to me! *(Calls off again)* Polk, attack the right flank! Go, man!

ROB
Those people are dying!

DOC
They're just play-acting, son!

ROB
I think that guy's bleeding!

DOC
Calm down! Henderson always brings ketchup packets!

(More gunshots, much closer. ROB lets out a girlish cry. DOC shouts orders)

DOC
When you're out of shot, fix bayonets and draw sabers!

ROB
Oh my god! They're coming right at us!

DOC
This is war, boy!

ROB
It's supposed to be pretend-war!

DOC
(To the unseen combatants) Die, you Yankee bastards!

(The battle surrounds them. ROB starts to really panic. He swings his saber like a man who has never done so before)

DOC
(to his opponents) This invasion of our sovereign land shall not be allowed! We shall fight you in the forests, we shall fight you in the hills! We shall fight you in the swamps, we shall...!*

(ROB, swinging wildly, accidently fake-stabs DOC. The battle grows quieter as the unseen fighters all stop and stare at what has just happened. Their voices can be heard)

VOICE 1
He just stabbed General Bragg!

VOICE 2
What the hell're you doin'?!

VOICE 3
That Yankee idjit just killed General Bragg!

VOICE 1
Stop the fight! Stop the damn fight!

VOICE 2
We can't stop! We're about to drive them back!

VOICE 3
Well, what the hell're we supposed to do?!

(DOC has been glaring at the shocked & confused ROB. Finally DOC, still holding ROB's saber, lowers

himself to the ground & "dies." ROB looks out at the unseen fighters)

ROB

I...I'm so sorry. *(Turns out to look at the men)* My bad.

(The sound of the men charging. ROB gets his arms up to defend himself. Blackout)

SCENE 3

(Lights up. Later that night. ROB's porch. DOC sits alone at first, clearly displeased. ROB soon re-enters, holding an icepack to his head. He sits down. They share a long uncomfortable silence. Finally--)

DOC
Thirty-five years.

ROB
I said I was sorry.

DOC
Thirty-five years.

ROB
You want me to say it again?

DOC
I've been a re-enactor for thirty-five years, never once in all that time did I witness such an atrocity.

ROB
Fine. OK. But I...

DOC
Even when Clayton O'Toole showed up to the Battle of Peachtree Hill completely inebriated, he still managed to carry himself with some semblance of dignity!

ROB
I feel like, at this point, I should point out that I was the one who got beat up.

DOC
Oh, you may have taken the odd lump, but make no mistake. I am the one bearing the scars of this battle.

ROB
Can you even hear yourself?

DOC
Can you?!

(ROB is silent)

DOC
Those people are my friends, my colleagues. And I looked all of them square in the eye and vouched for you. My god, I must've been out of my mind.

ROB
I never asked you to do this.

DOC
Of course you did. You moved in next to me.

ROB
That wasn't an invitation for you to drag me into this...whatever the hell this is.

DOC
It's called being neighborly, Robert. But I reckon

that's a foreign concept to you.

(Beat)

ROB
And just how is that a foreign concept to me?

DOC
I'm going home. Thank you for driving us to the field. Please give my regards to Madeline…

ROB
You want to say something to me, Doc? Here I am.

DOC
A gentleman doesn't disparage his host.

ROB
It's just you and me.

DOC
Yes, and fortunately one of us is a gentleman.

ROB
How is that not disparaging me?!

DOC
I never said which one of us I was referring to.

ROB
You think I can't see through this? I'm not an idiot, you know.

DOC
I say good evening.

ROB
You can stand there and smile and laugh and just…ooze this Southern charm, but I'm not an idiot, and I'm not deaf.

DOC
I'm sure I have no idea what you're talking
about.

ROB
I can hear all the little digs you throw at me.

DOC
Well, I never!

ROB
Come on! The stabs at Detroit, and sewing, and
Madeline...

DOC
That's quite enough! I've never said a thing about
your darling wife.

ROB
When you introduced us to...what's his name...
Buddy something...

DOC
Buddy Maddocks.

ROB
He asked if Maddie was my daughter!

DOC
And I corrected him!

ROB
Right, after you laughed for like two minutes.

DOC
My god. Are all Michiganians as dour and humor-
less as you?

ROB
It's "Michiganders" and you know it!

DOC
I have shown you nothing but hospitality, and you repaid me with humiliation.

ROB
It was an accident!

DOC
Was it? Or was it another Yankee trying to stick it to the South?

ROB
Come on!

DOC
Oh, I've seen your type before. You think we're all ignorant rednecks. We couldn't possibly be as smart and cultured as our enlightened Northern brethren.

ROB
You're going to want to back off.

DOC
Does it feel good, Robert, looking down your nose at us Southerners?

ROB
I don't have a problem with Southerners, Doc.

DOC
Oh? Indeed?

ROB
I have a problem with you.

(Beat. DOC silently rages)

ROB
You can call it "hospitality" all you want, but from

where I'm standing, it looks like you're trying to humiliate me. And I'll tell you this right now, I am not a man to mess with. You get me?

DOC
Sir, I pray that is your concussion talking. Because you do not want to make an enemy of Benjamin W. Boggs.

ROB
Yeah, what are you gonna do? Smother me in your rancid preserves?

DOC
You leave my preserves out...! *(Collects himself, still furious)* I gave my word to your dear wife that I will endeavor to help you. And that I shall do. But know this, Robert. There is a line between we two, and you were the one who crossed it. Good evening to you.

(DOC starts to walk off. ROB calls to him)

ROB
Hey! Don't do me no favors!

(ROB storms in, slamming the door. DOC smiles)

DOC
Oh, I've got a favor for you all right. Thirty-five years.

(He exits. Lights fade)

Scene 4

(The next morning. ROB is downstairs, eating cereal and still angry. MADDIE enters, dressed for work)

MADDIE
Hey, there you are. I *(She sees him eating)* …Honey?

ROB
Yeah?

MADDIE
Why are you eating breakfast outside? Are you watching Doc's house?

ROB
When the attack comes, it'll come from there.

MADDIE
Oh, boy,

ROB
It's quiet out here, Maddie. Too quiet.

MADDIE
It was just a misunderstanding.

ROB
(Noticing he's out of Cookie Crisp) Dammit.

MADDIE
I bet Doc isn't even thinking about it anymore.

ROB
Oh, he's thinking about it. Sitting there drinking a mint julep and twirling his big Georgia moustache and…

MADDIE
He called.

ROB
Who called?

MADDIE
Doc.

ROB
Did he want you to get out of the house before he opens fire?

MADDIE
He found you a job.

ROB
What?

MADDIE
It's with the guy we met yesterday…Buddy something.

ROB
Wait, wait, wait. What kind of job are we talking about here?

MADDIE
He said it was in automotives.

ROB
You gotta be kidding me.

(She hands him a piece of paper)

MADDIE
He said you had to come in today, to meet with the boss. It's on the corner of Main and Church Street.

ROB
What am I doing?

MADDIE
He didn't say. He just said to come in at nine.

ROB
Nine?! Hon, it's 8:30! Why didn't you tell me?!

MADDIE
You were in the shower!

ROB
I need pants! *(He jumps up, pantsless. He grabs MADDIE, hugging her. She smiles at him)*

MADDIE
So, which one of us was right about Doc? Was it me? 'Cause it feels like it was me.

ROB
Could you pick up some more Cookie Crisp on the way home? *(Runs offstage)*

MADDIE
Go kick butt today, baby! Baby?! *(He's gone)* That's my man.

(Lights change)

SCENE 5

(In the darkness, the sounds of phones ringing. As lights rise, ROB can be seen answering them)

ROB
Maddocks Toyota, Rob speaking. How can I help you? Please hold. *(ROB stares at the phone, unsure how to work it)* OK. OK. You can do this. It's just a phone. *(He hits a button and talks into the receiver)* Buddy, you've got a call on... *(He quickly realizes he's not on the intercom. He tries to make sure he hasn't hung up on the caller)* Hello? Are you still...hello? *(He hung up on them. He's also hit the intercom without realizing it)* Stupid piece of crap phone... *(His voice booms over the dealership. He madly scrambles to turn off the intercom)* Oh god. Sorry....everyone...sorry... *(He manages to turn off the intercom. He seethes in quiet rage and tries to calm himself)* ... calm blue ocean, calm blue ocean... *(The phone rings again. He answers)* Maddocks Toyota. Rob Speaking, how can I... Yeah, sorry about that. It's my first day and...Mm-hmm...Mm-hmm...Ah,

from Michigan, actually. Mm-hmm...Please hold. *(ROB puts the customer on hold, then stares at the phone, again unable to figure out how to work the intercom)* Ah, the hell with it. *(He shouts across the room)* Hey, Buddy! You've got a call on line one! *(He sits back down at his desk, defeated. He rests his head on the desk, then slowly grabs some scissors, making as though he might stab the phone)*

(MADDIE enters. She is singing something to the tune of 9 to 5 by Dollar Parton. She has lunch with her)

MADDIE
Workin' 9 to 5, 'cause my husband is so awesome...Workin' 9 to 5, something else that rhymes with awesome...

(ROB rises and hugs her)

MADDIE
How's it goin', working man?

ROB
It's goin'.

MADDIE
This is great! Look at you, back in the mix!

ROB
Honey, I'm a secretary.

MADDIE
Oh. You're not covering for someone 'til...?

ROB
Oh no. No no no. *(He taps the sign on the desk that reads ROB GRAFF)* This desk is aaaallll mine. And the beauty...THE BEAUTY of it is, they figured that, with my experience, I only

needed one hour of training.

MADDIE
Honey...

ROB
This phone...the space shuttle doesn't have this many buttons!

MADDIE
You're getting loud.

ROB
(Quiets down, trying to reign himself in) He said "automotive", right? That's what he said?

MADDIE
What?

ROB
That's what Doc Boggs said to you, yeah?

MADDIE
Oh. Yeah.

ROB
(to himself) ...very nice, you crafty son of a...

MADDIE
It's just your first day.

ROB
This is his opening salvo. And it's brilliant.

MADDIE
You're losing me.

ROB
He knows I need this job. He knows I'll just sit here and take the humiliation because...

MADDIE
Rob.

(He stops, looks at her)

MADDIE
Honey, I love you. But calling your new job "humiliating" on the sales floor is maybe not a great idea.

(He clearly wants to say more, but keeps his mouth shut)

MADDIE
I...brought you lunch? *(She opens the bag)*

ROB
Oh my god, that smells amazing.

MADDIE
It's from this little barbeque place next to my office.

ROB
Thank you.

MADDIE
And...look! *(She takes a slice of pie out of the bag)*

ROB
Oh my god. Please tell me that's pecan pie.

MADDIE
Just for you, babycakes.

ROB
Best wife ever.

MADDIE
Is it ok if we eat together? Or should I...?

ROB
(Calling over her head) Buddy, am I cool to take

my lunch now? *(Buddy agrees)* Yeah, we're good. There's a picnic table outside and...

(Just as they start to head out, DOC enters. He is very pleased with himself)

DOC
Well now! Look at the happy couple.*(He kisses her hand)* Madeline. *(He offers his hand to ROB. Smiles)* Robert.

(ROB grudgingly shakes it)

DOC
I was in the neighborhood and thought I might check in on you.

ROB
Awesome.

DOC
Do you find this situation to your liking, Robert? I know it's not the assembly line, but...

ROB
I didn't work the assembly line. I was an engineer.

DOC
Oh. My mistake. I'm afraid the distinction is lost on an old sawbones like me.

MADDIE
He's settling in nicely. Aren't you, Rob?

ROB
Yuh-huh.

DOC
Excellent! And Robert, there's no need to thank me.

ROB
OK.

DOC
After all. I was only being neighborly. Ooh, what have we here? *(Notices their lunch)*

MADDIE
I brought Rob lunch.

DOC
Do my nostrils detect the enticing aroma of Miss Cody's Homestyle Barbecue?

MADDIE
Oh. Actually, yeah.

DOC
An excellent choice, Madeline. There are few things I savor more than her pulled pork in my mouth.

(Beat. ROB is trying hard not to laugh)

DOC
Did I say something funny, Robert?

ROB
Nope.

DOC
Well, I won't keep you from your well-earned repast. Y'all have a lovely… *(He gets the slightest bit dizzy, stabling himself on ROB's desk)*

MADDIE
Are you alright?

DOC
Oh, nothing to concern yourself over. I'm just a bit winded is all. Walking down to the dealership

must've taken more out of me than I'd guessed.

MADDIE
You should sit down.

DOC
No, no. It's all right. *(He chuckles a little)*

ROB
What is it?

DOC
Well, in my haste to get started this morning, I must've skipped my breakfast. My blood sugar must be low is all.

(MADDIE checks his pulse)

MADDIE
Your heart's racing. Just sit down.

(He does so. MADDIE opens the lunch bag and pulls out the slice of pie)

ROB
Whoa. What're you doing?

MADDIE
He needs something sweet, to get his blood sugar up.

ROB
OK. Fine. There's a gumball machine right over...

DOC
I don't want to be a bother.

MADDIE
A gumball isn't gonna do it, Rob.

ROB
But...it's my pie.

DOC
Perhaps if I just rest my eyes…

MADDIE
I can get you more on my way home.

ROB
Right. I know. I just…it's been a rough day and…

MADDIE
Honey.

(She looks at him. ROB stares at her, then to DOC. DOC smiles sweetly. ROB hands the piece of pie to DOC)

ROB
Here you go.

DOC
Well, I do appreciate it.

MADDIE
It's nothing.

DOC
No, no. It's an act of kindness, one I'll not soon forget.

ROB
So I guess we're even.

DOC
Well, if you think that a piece of pie is of equal value to finding you a job, then…

ROB
Just…enjoy it.

DOC
Don't mind if I do. *(DOC takes out a napkin, tucks*

it into his shirt, gets a fork, and takes a bite. He savors it, smiling) Now. That is good pie. *(He continues to eat, smiling. Lights fade)*

SCENE 6

(Later that night. MADDIE is still cleaning/unpacking. ROB enters with an armful of library books)

MADDIE
Hey, baby.

ROB
Hey.

(They kiss. ROB sets the books on the table and starts to go through them)

MADDIE
Those are books.

ROB
Yuh-huh.

MADDIE
I thought you were getting mosquito netting.

(While reading, he sets a small paper bag on the table)

MADDIE
Honey?

ROB
Yeah?

MADDIE
Why do you have... *(She picks up one of the books)*
Chattanooga: A Death Grip on the Confederacy?

ROB
He thinks I'm gonna roll over and surrender.
That's his first mistake.

MADDIE
Who?

ROB
Doc Boggs. He's a crafty old bird, I'll give him
that. But...

MADDIE
Rob, what are you doing?

ROB
Don't you see? It's all part of a plan! Making me
a secretary was only step one. He's got this weird
revenge-kick going on.

(Beat)

MADDIE
I'm guessing you can't hear how crazy you sound
right now.

ROB
I'm sitting there today, answering these phones,
and it hits me. If I'm going to strike back at him,
I've got to be smart about it. So why not do the
last thing he'd expect me to do?

MADDIE
Act like a sane person?

ROB
No! Study up on Civil War battles, but from the Northern side. That's his blindspot, honey! See what I'm saying?

MADDIE
Not…entirely.

ROB
He's got zero respect for the Union. So when my counter-attack comes, he won't…

MADDIE
Honey. Stop.

(He stares at her)

MADDIE
You're turning this into something it isn't.

ROB
But…but…counter-attack…

MADDIE
Doc hasn't done anything to you, except help you get a job. I know you've got this…intense competitive streak, but…

ROB
I do not!

MADDIE
Red Wings at the playoffs.

(Beat)

ROB
Go on.

MADDIE

I've seen you take things personally when they aren't. This is one of those times. I'm saying this 'cause I love you, and I really, really don't want you to burn down Doc's house.

ROB

I wasn't going to burn down his house!

MADDIE

*(Holds up another book)*You checked out Sherman's March. That doesn't inspire confidence.

ROB

I just...you weren't there, OK. He threatened me.

MADDIE

Then why did he get you a job?!

ROB

To put me under his thumb! I'm telling you, this is just the beginning! I don't know what's coming next, but it's be gonna worse, more humiliating than...

MADDIE

Stop! He's our neighbor, ok? He's our one friend here. Just let it go. You guys got off on the wrong foot. I'll give you that. But he's a nice old man who's just trying to help us get settled. I promise you.

(ROB stares at her. Finally--)

ROB

Jeez, I was really heading for the deep end, wasn't I?

MADDIE

Without water wings.

ROB
Sorry about that. I just...it was a rough day.

(She sits with him, holds him)

MADDIE
I know, honey. But we just moved in. Give it a little time.

ROB
I know. Yeah. Just need to focus on the positive.

MADDIE
Now, see? That's sensible-Rob. I like sensible-Rob. I like to kiss sensible-Rob.

ROB
Sensible-Rob likes that too.

(They kiss. She rises)

MADDIE
I'm gonna hit the shower. Wanna join me?

ROB
Let me finish working on the porch. I'll be up in a bit.

MADDIE
OK. Love you.

ROB
I love you too.

(She heads upstairs. ROB watches her go. When he's confident that she's gone, he cracks open the books again)

ROB
Let's do this.

(Lights fade)

SCENE 7

(Lights change. What follows is a quick montage of scenarios, over the course of several weeks, detailing ROB & DOC's continued battle. When Johnny Comes Marching Home plays underneath. Between each scenario is the sound of a single shot fired. ROB comes home, wearing goggles. He speaks to himself)

ROB
Know what, Doc? That peach tree is close to my property line. Too close.

(Bang. Lights up on DOC)

DOC
Well Rodney, I think 9pm is a little late to be running a chain saw. Perhaps you could drive by in your squad car and ask him to keep it down. Thank you, Rodney.

(Bang. MADDIE & ROB at home)

MADDIE
What you got there?

ROB
Fox pee. Scares away raccoons and possums...
(MADDIE exits) and smells mighty good on your
neighbor's Camry.

(Bang. MADDIE and DOC at the supermarket)

MADDIE
Weird, animals don't usually mark their territory
on cars.

DOC
I can think of one animal that might.

MADDIE
Huh, they're all out of Cookie Crisp, that's Rob's
favorite.

DOC
Yes, I believe you mentioned that. *(MADDIE
exits)* And now they're my favorite too.

*(Bang. ROB is at the dealership, he speaks with
Buddy)*

ROB
Hey, Buddy! Is this the work order for Doc Boggs
Camry? Yeah, I'll put it right through, no problem.
(crumples up the paper) Call the cops on me will ya?

(Bang. DOC & MADDIE speak on the phone)

DOC
Oh, well... you see, I dropped my van off at the
dealership nearly a week ago, and it turns out
they're still waiting on a part. And sadly I don't
have another vehicle so...

MADDIE
So...wait. How are you getting around?

DOC
Well, frankly, I'm not.

MADDIE
Why didn't you say so? Would you like to borrow
Rob's car?

DOC
Oh, I couldn't do that.

MADDIE
It's not a big deal. I can drive him in to the dealership on my way to work.

DOC
Well, if you're sure it wouldn't be a problem.

MADDIE
Doc, I insist.

(There's a beep. MADDIE looks at her phone)

MADDIE
Speak of the devil. Rob's on the other line.

DOC
Well, you tell him I said thank you for the loaner.
I'll take good care of his vehicle.

MADDIE
You bet.

DOC
And thank you again for tending to Barksdale.

MADDIE
No problem. Goodnight, Doc.

DOC
And to you.

(Bang. Lights down on DOC. Rise on ROB)

MADDIE
Hey, baby.

ROB
Hey, I'm thinking of picking up a pizza on the way home. You in?

MADDIE
I am so very, very in. But go ahead and start without me. I'm heading over to Doc's.

ROB
Uhm...why?

MADDIE
Nothing serious. His bulldog's arthritis is acting up. I'm just gonna drop off some Rimadyl.

(Beat. ROB smiles at this)

ROB
Doc has a dog?

(Bang. The next day. ROB is at home, still working on the porch)

DOC
Graff!

(DOC enters, furious. ROB sits up)

ROB
What's up, Doc?

DOC
Explain yourself.

(Beat)

ROB
Really? You've never seen Bugs Bunny?

DOC
Don't you barb with me, boy! You know damn well what I'm talking about!

ROB
I do?

DOC
Explain to me why, when I returned home from my Historical Society meeting, I was greeted by my beloved Barksdale...WEARING THIS! *(He slams a small dog costume on the table. ROB examines it. It's a New York Yankees costume)*

ROB
Maybe Barksdale likes their chances this year.

DOC
That dog would never root for anyone but his beloved Braves! This costume is an outrage!

ROB
Sounds to me like you should be talking to him.

DOC
Do you think me a fool, sir?

ROB
Nope.

DOC
I know exactly where this...outfit came from. You crept into my home, and took advantage of my sweet canine's gentle and trusting nature.

ROB
(Straightening up and walking right up to DOC, nose to nose) Prove it.

(DOC doesn't flinch, but smiles a sinister smile)

DOC
Boy, you're too young a kitten to fool an old cat like me.

(ROB backs off a little)

DOC
These little skirmishes between us, they've provided a nice distraction. I'll give you that. But what I say now, I say for your own benefit. Desist. You are perilously close to awakening a sleeping bear. And this bear has claws you have not yet seen.

(Beat)

ROB
So…wait. Are you a cat or a bear?

DOC
(Storming out, he stops at the door) This isn't over, boy. Oh no. Not by a country mile.

(DOC leaves, slamming the door. ROB grabs a beer from the fridge, opens and drinks)

ROB
You got that right.

(Bang. Lights fade)

SCENE 8

(A few days later. The park, just before another re-enactment battle. DOC is there, putting on the last of his outfit. They are re-enacting The Battle of Perryville. As DOC prepares himself mentally for the battle, he waves to the occasional, unseen participant)

DOC
(muttering to himself) ...good god, it's a hot one...

(ROB enters, wearing a full Union soldier's uniform)

ROB
Good thing the battle hasn't started yet. I'd love to tell my commanding officer that I captured General Braxton Bragg.

DOC
Graff.

ROB
Boggs.

DOC
What the hell do you think you're doing?

ROB
Really? You can't tell?

DOC
Am I to assume you've joined the Union's cause?

ROB
I'd like to think I traded up.

DOC
Traded up?! This is the Battle of Perryville, boy!
A resounding Confederate victory!

ROB
Well, yes and no.

DOC
Yes and...?! My god, the sheer hubris! We stopped
Buell's advance! AND captured over 4,000 Union
troops. We...

ROB
Retreated.

(DOC stops, flustered and stammering)

ROB
Oh yeah. That's right. This dumb Yankee knows
how to read. Bragg had real victory in his hand,
and what did he do, Doc?

DOC
It...it was a strategic withdrawal! He...I...

ROB
He got word that the other Confederate armies
around him had gotten SPANKED by the Union.
He knew that, even if he kept Perryville, he'd be
surrounded by the enemy. So against the advice
of two of his own generals, he turned tail and ran.

(DOC just glares at him)

ROB
One of his own soldiers said...hold on...*(Riffles
through his pockets, finding his notes)* Here we
go..."Bragg showed a perplexity and vacillation
that had become simply appalling."

DOC
That may be factually accurate, but...

ROB
But nothing! See, I've decided to play the long
war here, Doc. I'm willing to lose the occasional
battle, 'cause I got my eye on the prize.

(The sound of gunfire. The battle is starting)

DOC
The battle's on, you idiot! Get out of...

ROB
It stings, doesn't it? Knowing that you're wearing
the name of a Loser! Oh, he enjoyed a win here
and there, but Bragg went down in flames!

DOC
(calling to his troops) McPherson! Shore your line
up to the East! They're gonna...

ROB
You started this war, pal, but don't forget who's
gonna win in the end!

DOC
Get out of here, Yankee Jim!

(ROB starts to sing badly, at the top of his lungs)

ROB
So we sang the chorus from Atlanta to the sea

WHILE WE WERE MARCHING THROUGH GEORGIA

(In a fit of anger, DOC stabs ROB. ROB just stands there)

DOC
You want to stay where you don't belong, don't be surprised if you get skewered.

(ROB glares at DOC)

DOC
You took a saber to the lung, son. Now be a good Yankee, lie down and die.

(ROB lies down, but refuses to remain silent. DOC is jubilant, but seems shaky and a bit unfocused)

DOC
We've done it! Beat those bastards back, men!

ROB
You can't stab the truth, Doc.

DOC
Sound the charge!

ROB
Your army is just a bunch of rednecks in matching pajamas.

DOC
Polk! Move those damn cannons!

ROB
The North won...

DOC
No!

ROB
...because they were smarter, better equipped and

just better fighters.

DOC
Be silent, corpse!

ROB
Don't hate me 'cause I'm right, grandpa.

DOC
You're not right! You're a rude, thoughtless punk working a woman's job!

ROB
Hey!

DOC
My god...you're a secretary and a seamstress! It would almost be funny if it weren't so damn sad.

ROB
(Rising) You are so lucky I don't hit senior citizens.

DOC
Back on the ground, Lazarus!

(ROB lies back down. As they argue, DOC starts to get noticeably weaker)

DOC
Your one and only achievement was somehow convincing a woman half your age to be your wife. And even she's more a man than you!

ROB
She's not half my age!

DOC
You're the poster child for midlife crisis, and you can't even see it.

ROB
At least I'm not a walking, talking stereotype!

DOC
How dare you!

ROB
I mean, do you wake up in the morning and ask yourself "How can I be more like Foghorn Leghorn?"

DOC
I am descended from philosophers and generals! I was raised in a time when breeding counted for something! When a man worked hard, provided for his family and treated every man...be he a stranger or relation..like they were his...neighbor...

(DOC has gone to one knee, clutching his chest. ROB hasn't noticed at first)

ROB
Like hell!

DOC
Oh Christ...my heart...

ROB
You've been riding my ass ever since...

DOC
Medic...call a medic...

ROB
Oh! Sorry! Corpses don't talk back, do they?

(DOC grabs ROB. ROB now realizes that something's wrong)

DOC
...Ambulance...damn you...

ROB
Holy...Doc? What's...?

DOC
It's...my damn...heart, you imbecile...

(DOC collapses to the ground, still conscious, but in rough shape. He grabs ROB's arm, but doesn't look at him)

DOC
I shall...rise again. *(He lets go of ROB and lies there)*

ROB
(Scared, unsure what to do) Medic...Medic!

(Lights fade)

END OF ACT ONE

ACT II

Scene 1

(The hospital. MADDIE & ROB are waiting. MADDIE has a bouquet of flowers. She's looking around)

MADDIE
God, are we the only ones here? *(Notices ROB's anxiety)* Honey, it's not your fault.

ROB
I know it's not my fault.

(Beat)

MADDIE
It's maybe a tiny, little bit your fault.

ROB
No it isn't.

MADDIE
You were antagonizing him. In 103 degree weather.

ROB
You don't know that.

MADDIE
I was in the stands.

ROB
There were...you know, things always look bad when you take them out of context, but...

MADDIE
I just...don't you even feel a little bad?

ROB
No. 'Cause he's faking it.

(Beat)

MADDIE
I don't think he's faking it.

ROB
Sweet, innocent Maddie.

MADDIE
I mean, if it was nothing, they would've released him already.

ROB
The guy's 102 years old. I'm not saying nothing's wrong with him. I'm just saying he didn't have a heart attack.

MADDIE
Rob...

ROB
It's Fort Macon all over again.

MADDIE
I get this feeling like you can't hear yourself talking.

ROB
It was this old fort that General Sherman turned into a prison. The conditions there were terrible. Eventually, the imprisoned solders started faking illness so they...

MADDIE
Rob!

(He stops talking)

MADDIE
Our neighbor had a heart attack. It happened.

ROB
I just...

MADDIE
It happened. And I need to know that, when we go in there, you're not going to...provoke him. OK?

ROB
What if he starts into me?

MADDIE
I don't care if he punches you in the face. You are NOT going to push his buttons, y'hear?

ROB
I'll be good.

MADDIE
OK. Let's go.

(Lights rise on the rest of the stage. DOC is lying in a hospital bed, comfortable & reading a book. He smiles when he sees them)

DOC
Well now. My day just got a little brighter.

MADDIE
Hello, Doc.

DOC
And a fine hello to you.

(She hugs him. ROB comes to him, unsure how to react)

ROB
Hiya.

DOC
Robert. Good to see you. *(Shakes ROB's hand, seemingly without any rancor)*

MADDIE
I hope we're not bothering you.

DOC
Not at all. It's a balm to my soul to finally have some visitors.

MADDIE
Are we the first people to visit?

(Beat)

DOC
And what do you have there? Lilies?

ROB
Oh. Yeah. Lemme just... *(Sets them on a table)*

MADDIE
They're from our garden.

DOC
I thought they might be.

ROB
You're not allergic or anything, are you?

DOC
To neighborly kindness? No, sir. I'd say it's just what the doctor ordered.

MADDIE
(Sitting with him) How are you doing?

DOC
Well, I'll tell you. They brought me in here all agitated, and it turned out to be nothin' but a little Atrial Flutter.

ROB
So not a heart attack?

DOC
Not exactly, no. Turns out my heartbeat just had a hitch in its step.

ROB
OK then.

MADDIE
So the prognosis is good?

DOC
I wouldn't go that far.

(Beat)

DOC
Looks like I'm gonna have to pass on the biscuits and gravy from this day forward. And for a life-long gourmand like myself, that's a serious prognosis indeed. Beware the Southern cuisine. It's put many a man in the ground.

(Beat. No one is entirely certain how to keep the conversation going)

DOC
Madeline, would you be so kind as to give me a moment with your husband?

ROB
What?

MADDIE
Of course.

ROB
What?

(She pats ROB on the arm as she leaves)

ROB
So...how about that...hospital food...?

DOC
Are you nervous, Robert?

ROB
(Laughing unconvincingly) What? No.

DOC
I'm just an old, bedridden man. You can cease your perspirations.

ROB
I'm fine, OK? *(Has seated himself on the other side of the room)*

DOC
Come closer.

ROB
I can hear you fine from here.

DOC
Come. Closer.

(ROB moves closer to DOC's bed)

DOC
Robert, Robert, Robert....we've made quite a mess.

(Beat)

ROB
Do...do you want me to get the nurse?

DOC
That's not what I meant, you...! *(Reigns himself in)* I'm a proud man. And I don't take kindly to folks rubbin' my rhubarb. That's not to say I'm without a sense of humor. But you have tested my patience, time and again.

(ROB wants to argue, but fights the urge)

DOC
However, geography has bound the two of us together. And as such, I must swallow my pride, and ask you to do me a favor. *(Grabs ROB's arm)* My dog, Robert. Take care of my dog.

ROB
Are you serious?

DOC
Barksdale...he's a good boy. But he's old, and he needs someone to take care of him.

ROB
You want us to take him?

DOC
Not unless you're overly fond of dog urine. He gets nervous in new places.

ROB
So...you want me to go to your house?

DOC
I don't have another choice! Please, you must do this for me.

ROB
I really think you'd be more comfortable with Buddy. Or that guy with the goiter.

DOC
They're not my neighbors, son! You're my neigh-bor. There is a sacred bond between us, and I'm asking you to honor that.

(ROB says nothing, hesitant)

DOC
I'm not asking so much. Just to feed him, to walk him...to keep him company. Of course, I would do it myself, but the events of yesterday have left me temporarily bedridden. Yes, yes. Yesterday took quite its toll. It surely did. I...

ROB
I'll do it.

DOC
And here's my key. *(Hands ROB his key)*

DOC
He takes a bowl of kibble at 7 in the morning, and another at 5 in the evening. And he needs to be walked at least twice a day. At least. And no outfits. Y'hear me?

ROB
Yes.

(DOC offers his hand. ROB shakes it. DOC grabs his arm)

DOC
You can insult a man all you'd like. But not his dog, Robert. Never his dog.

(Lights fade)

Scene 2

(DOC's house. ROB is sitting in a chair, holding a photo. A knock on the door. An old dog can be heard sort-of barking offstage)

MADDIE
Rob?

ROB
Barksdale, no. Barksdale...just... *(Calls offstage)* It's unlocked! *(Back to Barksdale)* It's not Doc, buddy. Just hang on...

(ROB goes off, opening the door. MADDIE enters)

MADDIE
Hey, honey.

ROB
Hey.

MADDIE
I got your voicemail. What's the problem?

ROB
He's not going outside! And he won't make a mess inside either! I'm worried his colon's gonna explode.

MADDIE
(Chuckling a little) Really? You don't get what's wrong here?

ROB
No!

MADDIE
Baby, you've got to go outside first.

(Beat)

ROB
For real?

MADDIE
For real.

ROB
But...but...the door's open.

MADDIE
Hon, this isn't unusual, not with a bulldog. They get really attached to people. He wants to be able to see you when he's outside. It makes him feel safe.

ROB
He's been going out there for years.

MADDIE
Yeah, probably with Doc standing out there with him the whole time.

ROB
So...I've got to watch him poop?

MADDIE
No, you just need to be within his line of sight.

(He stands there unconvinced. MADDIE takes the door from him)

MADDIE
Go on, get. Scoot.

ROB
Fine. *(Exits. He can be heard from outside)* Barksdale. Get your wrinkled butt out here. *(The sound of a dog dashing outside)* Holy crap! It worked!

MADDIE
Told you.

ROB
Oh man...you just saved this dog's life. I think he's been holding it in all day.

MADDIE
Rob! Why didn't you call me before?

ROB
I kinda got...Can I come inside?

MADDIE
Not unless you wanna give Barksdale a panic attack. Just wait.

ROB
Seriously, this is gonna take a while.

MADDIE
Then just wait. *(Looks around the house. She eventually finds the photo that ROB had. ROB can be heard offstage still)*

ROB
You can't still be going! *(The dog barks)* Ok, ok!

MADDIE
Dogs can sense when you're judging them.

ROB
Awesome. *(Barksdale can be heard running inside)*
How the hell does a dog that small hold so much
poop?

MADDIE
They're big eaters.

ROB
Honestly. I think I'm kind of impressed.

(ROB enters)

MADDIE
Is he ok?

ROB
Yeah. Went right to his dog bed. *(He sits with her)*
Why do they do that thing?

MADDIE
What thing?

ROB
That thing where they spin around before they
lie down.

MADDIE
It's just something they do.

ROB
It's kind of...

MADDIE
Cute?

ROB
I...yeah.

MADDIE
I told you he's a good dog.

ROB
There's something about that wrinkly, snaggle-
tooth face. I admit it. You should've seen him in
the Yankees outfit.

MADDIE
In the what?

ROB
What'cha got there?

(She holds up the picture)

ROB
Yeah, that's what I was trying to tell you. I didn't
call before because...

MADDIE
Because you were snooping through Doc's house.

(Beat)

ROB
No. Because it's not snooping when you're invited.

MADDIE
Is this Doc?

ROB
Yeah, probably twenty years ago.

MADDIE
Then who is she?

ROB
His daughter?

MADDIE
He has a kid?

ROB
I don't know. I was hoping maybe he told you.

MADDIE
Not a word.

ROB
It gets weirder.

MADDIE
Yeah?

ROB
That's the only picture I found of her. There isn't
another one, even in the attic.

MADDIE
Oh my god! You went into the attic?

ROB
I'm a very thorough dogsitter.

MADDIE
Rob...

ROB
I just wanna know, ok? I feel like there's a clue here.

MADDIE
A clue to what?

ROB
To why he hates me!

MADDIE
He doesn't hate you!

ROB
Come on. We've been after each other for two

months. You know this. He's only nice to me
when you're around, so that you don't figure out
what's going on.

MADDIE
Fine. What's going on?

ROB
War. This is war.

MADDIE
Then I'm ending it.

(He stares at her, ready to argue)

MADDIE
Whatever's going on between you two, it's got to
end.

ROB
Look. I didn't start this.

MADDIE
I don't care. I do. Not. Care. When someone ends
up in the hospital, then it's time to stop.

ROB
He said he was fine.

MADDIE
Yeah, this time. But he's an old man, he's retired,
and he has no friends.

(Beat)

ROB
What?

MADDIE
I just...Rob, people hate Doc.

ROB
Like hell. He's got all his buddies in the Civil War re-enactors, and...

MADDIE
When he brought Barksdale in, the guys in the office starting talking. They couldn't believe we were neighbors. Hon, Doc didn't want to retire. He had to. No one would go to him anymore.

ROB
Come on.

MADDIE
It's true. People would drive twenty minutes out of their way to go to another doctor. They say he's been this way for years.

ROB
And what way is that?

MADDIE
Come on. You know.

ROB
You're right. I do know. And I want to hear you say it.

MADDIE
I think...maybe you're not totally wrong about him, OK?

ROB
I want you to know that I could totally gloat right now, but I'm taking the high road. What I want to know is why you couldn't admit it 'til now.

MADDIE
Because he's all alone, and I wanted to be his friend. I think he's trying to change, Rob. I

mean...he gave us peach preserves.

ROB
Oh my god. I get it now. It all makes sense.

MADDIE
What?

ROB
Why he's been making my life hell. It's a classic reversal. He knows no one likes him. And all of a sudden, this Yankee moves in. He knows that, if he jumps on the Yankee-Hate-Wagon first, he'll get on everyone's good side. That clever bastard...

MADDIE
That sounds kind of nuts.

ROB
I know! He's totally mental.

MADDIE
No, I mean...

ROB
Oh my god, I gotta ask Buddy about this.

MADDIE
I thought Buddy hated you.

ROB
He hated me before 'cause we had nothing in common. But now...if he hates Doc like everyone else does...

MADDIE
No. No. Stop it.

ROB
Honey! This is my chance to fit in here! You gotta

give me this.

MADDIE
Not a chance.

ROB
I've been waiting for months! Listening to every snide comment, watching people laugh at my license plate. But now...now there's common ground.

MADDIE
Rob. Listen to yourself. You're talking about ganging up on a sick old man to make yourself feel better. That is wrong on so many levels.

ROB
I...no, that's an oversimplification...

MADDIE
Go home.

ROB
What?

MADDIE
You need to go home. I'll take care of Barksdale.

ROB
Doc asked me to.

MADDIE
Because he's trying to rebuild the bridge. Clearly, that isn't what you want, so go home.

(Beat)

ROB
Fine. *(He storms out. MADDIE sits on the couch. Barksdale begins to whimper offstage. MADDIE rises, heading offstage to him)*

MADDIE
It's OK, little guy. He'll be back soon.

(Lights fade)

Scene 3

(Back at the hospital. It's night time. DOC is lying in the bed, watching TV with little interest. He has a cup of Jello. ROB enters)

DOC
What happened to my dog?

ROB
He's fine. Maddie's there right now.

DOC
Did something happen?

ROB
No. She's just...being neighborly. *(Sits next to DOC)* So you get to go home tomorrow, yeah?

DOC
That's what they tell me.

ROB
Too bad. Bet you're gonna miss flirting with the nurses. Am I right?

(DOC just stares at him)

ROB
I just…it was a joke.

(DOC eats his Jello)

ROB
Doc, what's your problem with me?

DOC
At the moment, you're interrupting my program.

ROB
All night, I've been going over this…thing between us. And it doesn't make sense. I mean, so I killed you on the battlefield. It was an accident.

DOC
Which incident are you referring to? When you stabbed me with your saber, or when you harangued me into a coronary episode?

ROB
Fine. You want me to say I'm a bad neighbor? I'm a bad neighbor. Are you happy now?

(Instead of fighting back, the question genuinely makes DOC think)

DOC
Happiness is a funny thing, Robert. *(Shakes off his reverie)* Why are you here?

ROB
I…don't really know. I wanted to come over, I guess.

DOC
Why? Were you going to put me in a Detroit

Tigers jersey while I slept?

ROB
No, I just...thought you'd want some company.

DOC
Well, you made the trip for nothing. I'll have you know that I was resting from a day full of visitors and well-wishers. In fact...

ROB
No you weren't.

DOC
Don't interrupt me, boy. I was just saying...

ROB
Doc, it's fine. You don't have to...it's fine.

(DOC just stares at him, then goes back to his Jello. ROB turns on the TV)

ROB
Bass Masters?

DOC
You know it?

ROB
I'm from the Great Lake State. I know from fishing.

DOC
Hmmm.

(They watch for a while)

ROB
Holy crap! Look at the size of that thing!

DOC
That's a fifteen-pounder if I ever saw one.

ROB
The way he was fighting it, I thought he had a pike or something.

DOC
No, no. A pike would jump more.

ROB
I don't know. I heard sometimes they go deep, to try and tangle the line.

DOC
What? Who told you that?

ROB
My dad.

DOC
Oh. Well.

(They watch in silence a little bit more. ROB gets up to leave)

ROB
You know, I'm just...I'm gonna head out. Take care of yourself Doc.

DOC
I always do.

(ROB exits as lights fade)

Scene 4

(ROB and MADDIE's house, a few days later. MADDIE is sitting at the table, lost in her own thoughts. ROB enters)

ROB
Hey, honey.

MADDIE
Hey.

ROB
I quit my job.

MADDIE
What?

ROB
This has been an extremely weird day.

MADDIE
What happened?

ROB
It starts out pretty normal. I'm answering phones, shooting the shit with Mark from maintenance. And Buddy comes over. He wants to ask me all about Doc. Someone told him I was dogsitting and...hon, you were right. He doesn't like Doc. Most of them don't. He wanted to know if he was out of the Re-enactors. Turns out Buddy's been gunning for the General Bragg spot for years. And I'm like "Hey, I thought you guys were all on the same team or something." Yeah, turns out the only reason they let Doc stay is because he started the entire Carson Community Re-Enactors in 1980. He's the only founding member left. No one's had the balls to kick him out, but now that he's sick, they figure...anyway, so he's sitting there, just dishing all this crap about Doc and...I don't know. I got mad. I don't know why, but...there were these people in the showroom, asking about one of the hybrids. And I just walk right over to them, tell them about Toyota issuing a recall on a bunch of their hybrids 'cause of the anti-lock brake software. And when I say I "told them", I mean top of my lungs. Like, people two blocks over could hear me. Then I go on a tear about the unintended acceleration recalls, the floor mat recalls...and yeah. That was that.

MADDIE
Wait. Did you quit, or did you get fired?

ROB
Um...kind of a grey area.

MADDIE
Oh my god.

ROB
Hon, I know it's sudden. I swear to you, I did not
go in today intending to quit. It just happened.
But I'll find something else. I promise. Mark asked
me to be his assistant coach at Little League this
year. I mean, that'll be fun, right? Next week,
he's taking the kids to Turner Field, and I get to
come! Honest to god, free trip to Turner Field!
We're gonna…

*(Beat. ROB realizes that MADDIE is just staring at
him)*

ROB
You're mad.

MADDIE
No.

ROB
I'm really sorry. I am. I just…I couldn't work
there anymore. Buddy's a total dick, and it
just…I want to do something else, you know?
That thing you were saying before, about being
able to do something else with my life. I think
you're right. Maybe this is my chance to start
over. Maybe I just need to…

MADDIE
Rob. I'm not mad. Really.

(He sits down next to her, takes her hands)

ROB
Baby? What is it?

(Lights fade)

SCENE 5

(DOC's house. ROB is sitting alone on the couch. He is alone with his thoughts for a while. After a moment, DOC enters and hands him a beer. DOC has a bottled water)

ROB
Thanks.

DOC
Well, I'm switching to red wine with dinner now, so why waste them?

ROB
Fair enough.

(They drink in silence for a bit)

DOC
So what brings you here, Robert? Surely you don't miss Barksdale that much.

ROB
Maddie's pregnant.

(Beat)

DOC
I see. Am I to assume this wasn't planned?

ROB
Yeah.

DOC
I see.

ROB
I mean…we wanted to have a kid, at some point. And…Christ, I'm 45 years old. Some point is now, isn't it?

DOC
That's one way to look at it.

ROB
It's just…now? Right now? Maddie's freaked out 'cause she just started this job that she loves, and she's already got to ask for maternity leave. She's worried that…

DOC
Don't worry about it.

ROB
Well, it's maybe a legit concern.

DOC
I'll make some calls. People 'round here owe me some favors. Perhaps I could…

ROB
Doc, I know.

DOC
Know what?

ROB
That you're…

DOC
What? I'm what?

ROB
Not the most popular guy in town.

(Beat)

DOC
Doesn't mean that I'm not owed some favors.

ROB
That's not what I came here for.

DOC
I know that. I'm simply offering to help.

ROB
You're not really offering though. You're just
going to go ahead and do it.

DOC
I'm not a thumb-twiddler, Robert. And I make no
apologies for that.

ROB
(Laughs a little) Man, we just can't stop pushing
each other's buttons, can we?

(DOC thinks on that, & laughs a bit himself)

DOC
You might be right about that.

(They drink in silence for a bit)

DOC
So what did you come here for?

ROB
Hmm?

DOC
You said you didn't come here for my favors. So
why then?

ROB
Because, as screwed up as it sounds, you're the
closest thing I've got to a friend in this town.

DOC
I'm fairly certain you didn't mean that to sound
as insulting as it did.

ROB
No, I didn't. Sorry.

DOC
It's all right, son. You've had a long day.

ROB
Yes I have, Doc. Yes I have.

(Beat. ROB finally gets to the heart of the problem)

ROB
My child is going to be born in Georgia.

(DOC stares at him)

ROB
Maddie's right about me. I've made pretty much
no effort to make this place my home. And now...
it's going to be my kid's home.

DOC
Is that such a bad thing?

ROB
No. Not in theory. It's just... There's a part of

me that's always had one foot out the door, you
know? Like...Maddie would get a job offer some-
where else, we'd sell the house...we'd go back to
Michigan or...I don't know. But...

DOC
Reality's setting in. This is your home now.

ROB
Oh god.

DOC
This is a nice town, Robert. In a nice state. You'll
come to see that. God willing and the creek don't
rise.

(ROB just stares at him)

ROB
I gotta be honest. I only understand maybe fifty
percent of your Southern...thingies.

DOC
It means "let's hope everything works out."

ROB
Oh. OK.

(Beat)

DOC
I'm going to tell you a story, Robert.

ROB
No, it's OK. You...

DOC
I knew a gentleman in medical school...Jim
Bodine...he was a Hoosier. He asked me one
time about Civil War Re-Enactments. Asked me

if the Confederates ever change the outcome of the battles, to allow ourselves to win. It was one of the single dumbest questions I've ever been asked. Y'see, we're not trying to rewrite history. We're trying to honor it. Jim...he had it in his head that we're all bigoted rednecks or some-such. It's the reason we often get so...defensive around Yankees. *(Gets them both another drink)* The South lost the war because we were in the wrong. Because we forgot we were all brothers, Blue and Grey and Black and White. Nowadays, we focus so much on the few things that divide us, that we constantly forget the multitude of things which unite us. It's like watching two grown men scream at each other, because one says donkey and the other says mule. In the end, they're still jackasses. If you'll pardon the collo-quialism.

(Beat)

ROB
Good beer.

DOC
I'm glad you enjoy it.

(They sit in silence again. ROB rises)

ROB
I should probably head back.

DOC
Oh.

ROB
I know you've only been home for a little bit. Probably want to get settled.

DOC
Of course.

ROB
But thanks again, for the beer. And for...yeah,
thanks.

DOC
You're welcome.

*(ROB goes to the door, but doesn't go. DOC notices
him staring)*

DOC
You want to ask me about Evelyn, don't you?

ROB
I...don't know who that is.

DOC
Yes you do. The young woman, in the picture you
took from my bedroom.

(ROB has no response. DOC smiles a bit)

DOC
You put her back on the wrong side of the
chifarobe, Robert.

ROB
Dammit. I thought so, but I wasn't sure.

DOC
It's all right.

ROB
I'm sorry if I...

DOC
She was my wife.

ROB
Oh. I didn't...really?

DOC
Yes.

ROB
But she's so...

DOC
Young?

ROB
Yeah.

DOC
You of all people should be sympathetic of that.

ROB
That's...fair.

DOC
She passed away. Almost twenty years ago.

ROB
Oh. I...I'm not sure what to say.

DOC
"Sorry" seems a paltry word, doesn't it?

ROB
Yeah.

DOC
I appreciate your sentiment, Robert. Yes, she was all of 32 when she passed. Heart aneurism. We'd only been together for five years. If you were wondering why I'm something of a...pariah in this town, that's why. I couldn't see past the injustice of it. It made me a difficult sort to be around.

(Gets his water) I doubt anyone intends to reach the end of their days alone. But it does happen. It shouldn't, but it does. *(DOC notices ROB staring at him, & smiles a little)* Do you expect me to go on, Robert? To bear my soul?

ROB
I...maybe?

DOC
I'm grateful for your attending to Barksdale. And for this visit. But let's face each other honestly. We are not the closest of friends, are we?

ROB
You got me a job as a secretary. For Toyota.

DOC
You broke into my house and played dress-up with my dog.

(Beat. They laugh)

ROB
Truce?

DOC
Truce.

(They shake hands. ROB starts to go)

DOC
Robert, I...could I request a favor of you?

ROB
Knock yourself out.

(DOC stares at him, not familiar with the expression)

ROB
Go ahead.

DOC
It's about the re-enactors.

ROB
Yeah, I should tell you right off, I think I'm done with that. It's a little too intense for me.

DOC
I understand. My physician has ordered me to resign my commission as well.

ROB
Oh. I'm sorry. I know that was kinda your thing.

DOC
Well, I'll still go, but only to watch. My battlefield days are over. *(Beat)* I hate Buddy Maddocks.

ROB
Yeah, so do I.

DOC
The arrogant upstart has been circling me like a vulture for years.

ROB
Yeah...he was after your part.

DOC
I'm well aware. He's left me two messages, trying to worm his way into my good graces.

ROB
Why?

DOC
It's a by-law I wrote into this county's Rules of Re-Enactment. Commanding officers can name their successors.

ROB
So he's trying to sweet-talk you into making him the new Braxton Bragg?

DOC
So it would appear.

ROB
That's insane! He doesn't have the discipline! Bragg was a by-the-book soldier. Buddy doesn't know Jefferson Davis from Jefferson Starship! *(Notices DOC staring at him)* I've been studying. This stuff is kind of addictive.

(DOC puts his hand on ROB's shoulder)

DOC
Yes it is, Robert. Yes it is.

(Lights fade)

Scene 6

(The battlefield. The sound of a crowd gathering, and "soldiers" getting ready. ROB enters, donning his new costume as Gen. Braxton Bragg. MADDIE is with him)

MADDIE
You look amazing.

ROB
I wish I'd had more time to take in the waist…

MADDIE
Stop fidgeting. It's un-Generally.

ROB
The hat doesn't look too big? *(She kisses him)*

MADDIE
It looks great. You look great.

ROB
I don't want to make a bad impression. This is a big deal.

MADDIE
Look at those people. They're not seeing Rob Graff anymore. They're seeing one of their own.

ROB
For today.

MADDIE
It's a start, honey.

ROB
I know. *(Beat)* Are you feeling ok? Do you wanna sit down?

MADDIE
And it begins.

ROB
I'm just saying.

MADDIE
Rob, I'm pregnant. I'm not an invalid.

ROB
Are you sure? I asked Doc to bring a wheelchair for you. And a hot compress for those swollen ankles.

MADDIE
You're so lucky you're in public right now.

ROB
Honey, don't get upset. The baby can sense that.

MADDIE
I owe you such an ass-kicking.

ROB
(Calling off to unseen "soldiers") Gentlemen, please remove this civilian from the battlefield. *(He sees that they're coming over)*

ROB
Guys, wait. Just kidding. Really.

(DOC has joined them)

DOC
Ms. Madeline, you look radiant.

MADDIE
Hi, Doc. *(She hugs him)*

DOC
Careful, now. I'm fragile.

MADDIE
Like hell.

ROB
(Offering his hand) Doc.

DOC
Robert.

(They shake hands, warmly)

DOC
The Confederate Stripes suit you well.

ROB
Thanks. The hat doesn't look too big?

MADDIE
Oh my lord.

DOC
You look every inch a commanding officer. How do you feel?

ROB
Well, the men and I went through the maneuvers one more time, just like you showed me. You should've seen Buddy's face when I told him he

has to die in the first wave. I read up on the battle last night, and...

DOC
Robert. How do you feel?

ROB
Oh. *(Thinks on that)* Good. I feel good.

DOC
All right then.

(A trumpet sounds)

DOC
Looks like they're gearing up. I don't want to keep you from your troops.

ROB
OK.

MADDIE
I brought us some sandwiches and Coke.

DOC
What kind of Coke?

MADDIE
Diet Sprite.

DOC
Aren't you a dear?

MADDIE
I surely am.

DOC
Now, Robert. I always found that a pep-talk before the battle really enhanced the enjoyment of the day. Something stirring, but not too long.

ROB
All right.

DOC
And don't forget. This is the Battle of Chattanooga.
The Army of the Cumberland will come charging
up that hill, guns a-blazing.

ROB
Yep.

DOC
And most importantly, you must call the retreat.
Can you do that, Robert? Can you lose the battle?

ROB
Doc. I got this.

DOC
(Claps ROB on the shoulder) I know you do, son.

MADDIE
Come here. *(She kisses him)*

ROB
Honey, not in front of the Army.

(She smacks his bottom, hard)

MADDIE
Go get 'em, General.

*(DOC & MADDIE walk off a little bit. ROB faces
the audience, his "soldiers")*

ROB
Ok, guys. Circle up. *(The crowd gathers)* Ok.
Yeah...so...here goes... Today, we are fighting
for our...um...brothers and sisters...who have
fought bravely...well, not our sisters...Not that
they couldn't, just that historically they... *(He*

stops, collects himself) I know you're probably as shocked to see me standing here as I am to be standing here. But it's important, I think. That we're all here, honoring the events as they happened. Not how they could have happened, but how they did happen. We're gonna lose today, fellas. But we're going to go down fighting. Together. We are fighting together. When they carry us from the field, they won't be carrying soldiers; they'll be carrying brothers. So...don't fear defeat. Just be proud, knowing that you have good men, brave men at your side. 'Cause that's how I'm gonna feel, out there with all of you. *(ROB raises his saber)* CHARGE!!!!

(The crowd cheers, lights fade)

Scene 7

(ROB & MADDIE's porch. The evening of July 4th. MADDIE is sitting on the porch by herself. She's on the phone with her mother)

MADDIE
No, he's still looking. Actually, nothing in auto-motives. I don't...mom. Mom. He just wants to try something else with his... 45 is not to... It's not. It's not. I'm just... OK. I'm just saying, everything's new for us here. So why not? We're going to be fine. I promise.

ROB
(Can be heard calling from inside) Maddie! There's a freaking bat in the kitchen! Holy crap! He's got a knife! You gotta do something!

MADDIE
Mom, I gotta go. Yeah, there are bats in Georgia too. Big ones. With attitudes. Love you. Bye. Bye. Bye. *(Hangs up)*

ROB
(Entering with a tray, three glasses, & a pitcher) Did it work?

MADDIE
Like a charm. She hates bats.

ROB
Everyone hates bats.

MADDIE
I don't hate bats.

(He just stares at her)

MADDIE
What? They've got those cute little scrunched up faces, and those big ears. They're like terriers with wings.

ROB
(Holds her) I love you 'cause you're weird.

MADDIE
You love me 'cause I'm awesome. And weird.

(They kiss)

ROB
Shiloh.

MADDIE
No.

ROB
Ulysses? Like Ulysses S...?

MADDIE
No.

ROB
What about Tyrus?

MADDIE
All signs point to "no".

ROB
But...no, hear me out. That was Ty Cobb's real name. And he was born in Georgia, but played for the Detroit Tigers, so we kinda have this "best of both worlds" thing.

MADDIE
I would maybe consider "Tyler". Also, it might not be a boy.

ROB
Totally fine. I have the perfect name if it's a girl.

MADDIE
I'm going to hate this, aren't I?

ROB
Robertina.

(Beat)

MADDIE
Honey, I'm going to need you to give me the baby name book. So I can burn it.
(A knock at the door. ROB goes for it)

ROB
Settle down, wifey. You're wisecracking for two now. *(He exits)*

MADDIE
How many ass-kickings do I owe you?

ROB
(offstage) Seven. *(Re-enters with DOC)*

DOC
Good evening, Madeline.

MADDIE
Hi, Doc. *(They hug)*

DOC
Oh my. Look at you. You've got the glow.

MADDIE
I do?

DOC
You most certainly do. It's very becoming.

ROB
Are you flirting with my wife?

DOC
If I were, you wouldn't stand a chance. *(Looks out at the view)* My goodness. I forgot how lovely the view is out here.

ROB
Is it that different than yours?

DOC
You've got a better view of the city, down there. Close enough to see it, but not so close that you can hear it.

ROB
You want some sweet tea?

DOC
You have sweet tea?

MADDIE
Yeah. Miss Cody gave me her recipe.

DOC
Well, I couldn't imagine a better teacher.

ROB
(Gives DOC a glass and grabs him a chair) Make

yourself comfortable already.

DOC
Don't mind if I do. *(DOC sits. ROB & MADDIE sit together)*

DOC
Quite a night, isn't it?

ROB
Yeah.

DOC
A little brisk, but lovely.

ROB
It's 82 degrees.

DOC
That's why I brought an overshirt. *(Beat)* While I appreciate the invitation, I'm not entirely certain why it was offered.

ROB
Just checking in. Saying howdy.

DOC
That's very kind of you.

ROB
(Shrugging) Besides, I didn't want you to miss the show.

DOC
What show?

(ROB waits, looking out over the horizon. Finally--)

ROB
Dammit. I was hoping it would start right then. The timing would've been incredible.

DOC
Madeline, am I missing something?

MADDIE
Give it a second. You'll...

(Suddenly, the stage fills with light as some fireworks go off)

ROB
There we go.

DOC
Oh. Oh my. I...I forgot what day it was.

MADDIE
You were right. It's a hell of a view.

DOC
Would you look at that. *(More fireworks go off. DOC just stares)* It's been a while since...thank you.

ROB
No problem.

DOC
It's lovely, isn't it? Just so...lovely.

ROB
You got that right.

(ROB & MADDIE smile, as they see DOC lost in the spectacle)

MADDIE
Happy 4th, Benjamin. *(She clinks his glass with her own)*

DOC
Oh. Yes, I...to you, as well, darling. And Robert.

(They watch the fireworks. After a while) Did you know I proposed to my wife on the 4th of July?

(They look at each other then back at the fireworks. Lights fade)

END OF PLAY

ABOUT THE PLAYWRIGHT

Joseph Zettelmaier is a Michigan-based playwright and four-time nominee for the Steinberg/American Theatre Critics Association Award for best new play, first in 2006 for ALL CHILDISH THINGS, then in 2007 for LANGUAGE LESSONS, in 2010 for IT CAME FROM MARS and in 2012 for NORTHERN AGGRESSION. Other plays include SALVAGE, THE GRAVEDIGGER - A FRANKENSTEIN PLAY, NORTHERN AGGRESSION, DR. SEWARD'S DRACULA, INVASIVE SPECIES, THE SCULLERY MAID, NIGHT BLOOMING, and EBENEZER.

POINT OF ORIGIN won Best Locally Created Script 2002 from the Ann Arbor News, and THE STILLNESS BETWEEN BREATHS also won Best New Play 2005 from the Oakland Press. THE STILLNESS BETWEEN BREATHS and IT

CAME FROM MARS were selected to appear in the National New Play Network's Festival of New Plays. He also co-authored Flyover, USA: Voices From Men of the Midwest at the Williamston Theatre (Winner of the 2009 Thespie Award for Best New Script). He also adapted CHRISTMAS CAROL'D for the Performance Network.

IT CAME FROM MARS was a recipient of 2009's Edgerton Foundation New American Play Award, and won Best New Script 2010 from the Lansing State Journal. His play NORTHERN AGGRESSION won the Edgerton Foundation New American Play Award in 2011.

Joseph is an Associate Artist at First Folio Shakespeare, an Artistic Ambassador to the National New Play Network, and an adjunct lecturer at Eastern Michigan University, where he teaches Dramatic Composition.

PLAYS BY JOSEPH ZETTELMAIER

IT CAME FROM MARS

EBENEEZER - A CHRISTMAS PLAY

THE GRAVEDIGGER
A FRANKENSTEIN PLAY
adapted from the novel by Mary Shelly

THE SCULLERY MAID

DEAD MAN'S SHOES

ALL CHILDISH THINGS

NORTHERN AGGRESSION
(*formerly* AND THE CREEK DON'T RISE)

For information about production rights, visit:

www.jzettelmaier.com

WILLIAMSTON ANTHOLOGY
VOL 1 & 2

Collecting 10 Years of Original Plays from Williamston Theatre
Including scripts by:
Annie Martin, Tony Caselli, Alan Gordan, Dennis E North,
Suzi Regan, Mark Sutton-Smith, & Joseph Zettelmaier

More Plays From SORDELET INK

A Tale of Two Cities
by Christoper M. Walsh
adapted from the novel by Charles Dickens

The Count of Monte Cristo
by Christoper M. Walsh
adapted from the novel by Alexandre Dumas

The Moonstone
by Robert Kauzlaric
adapted from the novel by Wilkie Collins

The Woman in White
by Robert Kauzlaric
adapted from the novel by Wilkie Collins

Season on the Line
by Shawn Pfautsch
adapted from Herman Melville's MOBY-DICK

Hatfield & McCoy
by Shawn Pfautsch

Once A Ponzi Time
by Joe Foust

The League of Awesome
by Corrbette Pasko and Sarah Sevigny

Eve of Ides
by David Blixt

Visit www.sordeletink.com for more!